Katy Duck
Dance Star

By Alyssa Satin Capucilli · Illustrated by Henry Cole

LITTLE SIMON
An imprint of Simon & Schuster Children's Publishing Division
New York London Toronto Sydney
1230 Avenue of the Americas, New York, New York 10020

Manufactured in the United States of America
2 4 6 8 10 9 7 5 3
ISBN: 978-1-4169-8279-1
These titles were previously published individually as Little Simon board books.

Katy Duck loved to dance.
She also loved to dress up.
When Aunt Ella sent a new rainbow-colored boa,
Katy wanted to wear it *everywhere*!

“This is what all the dance stars wear!” said Katy.
“Tra-la-la! Quack! Quack!
Tra-la-la! I’m a star!”

Katy glided through the museum.
"Tra-la-la! Quack! *Whoa!*"
"Do be more careful,"
said Mrs. Duck.

"I'm a star," said Katy,
whirling through the park.
Katy bent and swayed.
"Tra-la-la! Quack! Quack!
Tra-la-la! Quack! *Ugh!*"

When it was time for dance class,
Mrs. Duck said,
"Let's leave the boa at home, Katy."
"But this is what all the dance stars wear," insisted Katy. "I have to wear it to dance class. I just have to!"

And she twirled and spun all the way to class.

The music began.
"Can you fly like a butterfly?" called Mr. Tutu.
Katy's arms began to flutter.
"Tra-la-la! Quack! *Oops!*"

No one flew like a butterfly at all.
Katy's boa was tangled everywhere!
"Oh, dear," whispered Katy Duck.

The music soared.
It was time to leap, leap, leap,
and turn and turn, but . . .
“Tra-la-la! Quack!” *Bump!*

"Tra-la-la! Quack!" *Thud!*
Katy's boa wrapped around the other dancers' legs.
"Stop the music!" called Mr. Tutu. "Stop the music!"

The class turned to Katy.
And just then Katy knew what she had to do.
"I'm very sorry," said Katy Duck. "I didn't mean to hurt anyone. I wanted to look like a dance star."

“Why, you don’t need a boa for that, Katy,” said Mr. Tutu.
“I bet if we start the music and get back to work,
we can fill this whole room with dance stars!
Are you ready, Katy Duck?”

"Tra-la-la! Quack! Quack!" said Katy.
She was ready, indeed!
"HOW I LOVE TO DANCE!"
And she did.

And then she carefully wore her new boa home.
Just like all dance stars who ride the bus.

Dancing on a great stage was just like
Katy Duck dreamed it would be.
"Tra-la-la! Quack! Quack!
How I love to dance!"

Katy Duck felt her arms begin to flutter.
Her feet began to pitter patter.
Katy leaped and twirled.
She stretched and swayed.
"Bravo!" cheered the crowd. "Bravo!"

The bright lights twinkled, just like the starry evening sky.
Katy loved to dance under that sky!

The music began.
Katy Duck looked right. The other dancers nodded.
She looked left. Mr. Tutu smiled.
Katy Duck looked up.

"Tra-la-la! Gulp! Gulp!"

"Places everyone!" called Mr. Tutu.
"Take your places please!"
The curtains opened.
There were bright lights.
There were costumes.
There was an audience.
An audience filled with people.
Lots of people.

Katy and her class practiced
and practiced.
Katy practiced in the morning
and the afternoon.

Katy Duck practiced every
night under the starry
evening sky.
At last it was time for the
big dance show.

One day at dance class Mr. Tutu said,
"I have a wonderful surprise. We are going to have a dance show.
There will be a great stage.
There will be bright lights and costumes.
There will be music. And there will be lots of applause!"
"Tra-la-la! Quack! Quack!"
Katy Duck could hardly believe her ears.
It was a dream come true!

Most of all, Katy Duck loved
to dance under the starry
evening sky.
"Tra-la-la! Quack! Quack!"

Katy leaped and twirled until
Mrs. Duck said,
"It's bedtime, Katy Duck."
Katy climbed into bed and
dreamed. She dreamed of
dancing on a great stage.

Katy Duck loved to dance.
She loved to dance in the morning.

She loved to dance in
the afternoon.

Katy Duck

Center Stage

By Alyssa Satin Capucilli   Illustrated by Henry Cole